GERONIMO
STILTON

Published by Sweet Cherry Publishing Limited
Unit 36, Vulcan House,
Vulcan Road,
Leicester, LE5 3EF,
United Kingdom

First published in the UK in 2018
2018 edition

ISBN: 978-1-78226-374-6

Text by Geronimo Stilton
Art Director: Iacopo Bruno
Graphic Designer: Laura Dal Maso / theWorldofDOT
Original cover illustration by Roberto Ronchi and Christian Aliprandi
Concept of illustration by Roberta Bianchi, produced by Carolina Livio, Riccardo Sisti, and
Valentina Grassini with assistance from Elisabetta Natella
Initial and final page illustrations by Roberto Ronchi and Ennio Bufi MAD5, Studio Parlapà and
Andrea Cavallini. Map illustrations by Andrea Da Rold and Andrea Cavallini
Cover layout and typography by Elena Distefano
Interior layout and typography by Elena Distefano, Rhiannon Izard, Kellie Jones and Amy Wong
Graphics by Chiara Cebraro
© 2013 Edizioni Piemme S.p.A., Palazzo Mondadori – Via Mondadori, 1 – 20090 Segrate
© 2018 English edition, Sweet Cherry Publishing
International Rights © Atlantyca S.p.A. – Via Leopardi 8, 20123 Milano, Italy
Translation © 2015, Atlantyca S.p.A.

Original title: *Una tremenda vacanza a Villa Pitocca!*
Based on an original idea by Elisabetta Dami

www.geronimostilton.com/uk

www.sweetcherrypublishing.com

Printed and bound in Turkey

Geronimo Stilton

WELCOME TO
MOULDY
MANOR

Sweet Cherry
Publishing

A Mouserific Birthday

My dear rodent friends, before I begin my tale, let me introduce myself. My name is Stilton, *Geronimo Stilton*, and I am the editor of The Rodent's Gazette, the most famouse newspaper on Mouse Island.

It all began like this...

What a story I have for you today! It all began on a Saturday morning. But not just any Saturday – it was my birthday!

I absolutely **adore** my birthday. I like to celebrate with my friends and receive cards and gifts. But most of all, I like to give **presents**! So I put on my best suit and got ready to go out.

7

I was planning a fabumouse party, and I wanted to get loads of surprises for all my friends.

The doorbell **RANG**. My heart leaped as I scurried to open it. Someone had come to wish me a **happy birthday**!

It was my cousin Trap, who tore through my mousehole like a tornado. "Germeister, aren't you going to wish me a happy birthday? You've forgotten all about my birthday, haven't you?"

"Wh-what?" I stuttered. "Today is *your* birthday? I was sure it was next week!"

WAAAAH!

Trap began to sob like a mouseling, spraying **TEARS** everywhere. Within moments, I was soaked to the fur.

"*Waaaah!* You forgot about my birthdaaaay! **Gerry Berry**, how could you? I never expected this from yoooouu! No one cares about meeee!" He wiped his eyes on the sleeve of my jacket and **BLEW HIS NOSE** on my tie.

I tried to comfort him. "Trap, I am so sorry. I thought it was next week … Let me make it up to you. Let's celebrate together! You know, today is *my* birthday,

TO-DO LIST FOR ~~MY~~ TRAP'S BIRTHDAY

* Reserve a restaurant for ~~my~~ Trap's party
The fanciest restaurant in New Mouse City! No pinching pennies!

* Buy party favours for the guests
Something classy! Don't get all cheap on me, you misermouse!

* Think about the decorations
Think fancy! I want beautiful streamers! Nothing shoddy, you cheapskate!

* Buy a gift for the birthday mouse – that's me, Trap Stilton! And I expect an expensive, tasteful gift! Nothing cut-price!

Remember, it's not the thought that counts, it's the price tag!

too. I was just about to go out and do a little shopping. Here's the list!"

Trap immediately stopped crying. He RIPPED the list out of my paws and started marking it up with a red pen. Then he snatched my wallet and all my credit cards.

"**I'll take these!** No cheaping it up today, okay, **Gerry Berry**? Remember, it's my birthday. Pinching pennies is prohibited!"

"I am not a penny-pincher!" I protested, offended. "Why, I'm

downright famouse for my **generosity!**"

For a second, I thought I saw a sly smile under Trap's whiskers. **"Humph! Let me be the judge of that, Cousinkins!"**

A DEAL THAT CAN'T BE MISSED!

As soon as we hit the streets, Trap raced ahead of me, waving my credit cards in the air. I trudged behind him, shouting, "Trap, give them back!"

Trap scampered into the first store. I noticed there were **TONS** of sales (fortunately for me!).

In the window, colourful banners announced a ten percent discount on shirts, a twenty percent discount on jackets, a thirty percent discount on jeans, a forty percent discount on ties, and a fifty percent discount on boots.

"See, I'm doing you a favour," Trap told me.

"Check out these sales! Think about how much you'll save on my present. This is your lucky day, Cousinkins! Now you can give me **lots** of presents instead of just one. Just don't be a **cheapskate**, okay?"

I tried to remind him that I am a generous rodent (sometimes even a little *too* generous).

But before I could squeak a word, he shoved a pair of **ridiculous green boots** into my paws. "Here, why don't you buy these for yourself? After all, it's your birthday, too! Never say that I'm not generous, Cousin!

Why, these are fifty percent off. Just think about how much money you'll save!"

I wanted to say that it was easy for him to be generous with *my* money! Besides, I really didn't need a pair of tacky green boots. But the salesmouse was already *cooing* in my ears.

"Oh, Mr. Stilton, these boots are **absolutely fabumouse**! They are just perfect with your outfit! You simply can't let this opportunity pass you by! Look, they're made of very shiny leather, with soft padding and a nonslip sole. The style is so sophisticated, all sewn by paw ... with silver spurs and real gold toes!"

It was too bad they weren't my size. But the salesmouse convinced me that a smaller size would be fine.

Green boots?

"You'll see how they stretch after a little wearing! You ab-so-lute-ly can't miss an opportunity like this!"

The salesmouse made me try them on,

14

even though I could tell they'd be too tight. And then I couldn't remove them – they were stuck on my paws! I tried everything I could think of to get them off, but nothing worked ...

The store manager told me, "This happened once before, in 1928. There's only one solution: freeze your paws!"

I've had lots of **humiliating** moments in my life. But putting my paws into an ice cream shop's freezer ranks among the worst!

When she saw that I couldn't take off the boots, the salesmouse shrieked, *"So, are you going to buy them or not?"*

My ears drooped with embarrassment. But what could I do? I had to say yes! "Um, well ... I guess I'll buy them. How much are they?"

When she told me the price, I thought I needed to scrape the cheese out of my ears.

ARE YOU GOING TO BUY THEM OR NOT?

I TRIED **EVERYTHING**
TO GET THE
BOOTS OFF MY PAWS!

I tried asking for more help!

Can you do it?

Argh!
Ooo
I tried kicking my paws in the air, but that just made the baby powder fall onto my snout!

I tried rotating my ankles, but I almost sprained them!

Ow!

By the way, this whole time, the boots were

BRRR.
The store manager told me to freeze my paws. How humiliating!

"Wh-what? That much?!"

But Trap squeaked up as if he were an official boot expert. "Listen to me! This is a real steal! These boots used to cost twice that much! Don't you realise how much you're saving?"

I had two choices: I could buy the boots, or I could cut off my paws. So I bought them, even though they were way too small!

Meanwhile, Trap was using my credit card to buy himself a mountain of presents. I didn't have the strength to protest: **my paws hurt too much!**

I tried walking on my toes, but that hurt even more. I tried walking on my heels, but I lost my balance and fell flat on my snout. I tried hopping on my left paw, then on my right, and then on both ... but nothing worked!

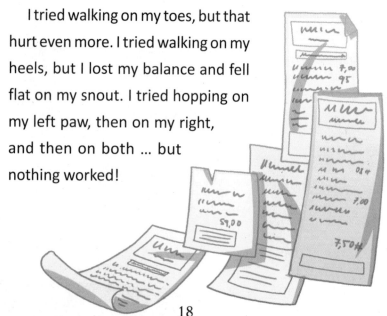

Finally, I gave up. I was just destined to have sore paws.

Trap dragged me from one store to another. He just bought and bought and bought. Then he tried to hide how much of my money he'd spent by **THROWING AWAY ALL THE RECEIPTS!**

TRAP'S PURCHASES

 MousePod, MousePad, MousePhone - including cases and battery chargers!

Pillows made of fake cat fur!

 flowered swimming trunks!

 MousePhone stand shaped like a werecat. Scary!

 Portable fridge in the shape of a mouse. It squeaks when you open it!

Pure gold, dishwasher-safe sunglasses!

 Toothbrush holders for him and her!

Golden egg cup, studded with crystals. Comes with a silver spoon!

 Set of porcelain plates with silver forks, designed by Louis Mouson!

Special cheese-scented, organic toilet paper!

SALE 0%   SALE 20%   SALE 30%   SALE 40%

Watch with built-in satellite feed!

Gold leisure suit ... because Trap is worth it!

Tissue box cover made from Persian cat fur!

Umbrella that turns into a shower!

Dress shirt with diamond buttons!

Cat-shaped USB drive!

Lunch box that plays the Mouse Island national anthem!

Elegant hat guaranteed to give the wearer a distinguished air!

Scottish kilt and bagpipes!

Pyjamas for every day of the week!

Dinner at Le Squeakery

Clinging to the excuse that it was his birthday, Trap kept on buying, buying, buying. Everything was on sale! Unfortunately, that meant I kept on **PAYING, PAYING, PAYING.**

Soon my cash was all gone, but Trap had conveniently remembered to bring my chequebook. Then I used up all my cheques and was forced to use my emergency

This is the last of my cash.

Here you go!

What a cat-astrophe!

credit card – the only one Trap hadn't already snatched!

All of a sudden, the sun was setting, and I realised I was late for my birthday dinner!

I gathered all of Trap's little packages, **medium**-sized packages, and **BIG** packages. There were so many of them that I had to call not one, not two, but *three* taxis to pick them up.

Then I rushed to the restaurant, where I had a reservation for dinner.

Because it was my special day, I had invited my whole family, all my friends, and all my colleagues to the most famouse, expensive, and delicious restaurant in New Mouse City: Le Squeakery.

Still claiming that it was really his birthday, Trap had invited a bunch of friends, too. This dinner was going to cost me a tail and a paw! But a birthday comes only once a year, right? And it's so wonderful to celebrate together!

When we entered the restaurant, everyone was already sitting at the table, waiting for us. Everyone we invited had come, and everyone cheered: "Happy birthday, Geronimo! Happy birthday, Trap!"

The restaurant's famouse chef, Saucy Le Paws, came to greet us in the fur. He was a **CHUBBY** mouse with a smiley snout and a joke always at the ready. Wiping his paws on his apron, he squeaked, "Good

evening, Mr. Stilton. What can I cook for you tonight? Spicy Swiss pie with **black truffles**, Parmesan pie with Russian caviar, or I also have a fresh mozzarella pie ..."

Good evening!

I licked my whiskers. "Saucy, please make us all those wonderful pies. My friends and I will gobble them up!"

"Yes, Saucy!" my friends cried. "Bring us the first piiiiiiee!"

Saucy Le Paws

We stuffed ourselves with exquisite, exclusive, and very expensive food all night long. At the end of the evening, Saucy brought out an enormouse cake covered with whipped cream, melted cheese, and tiny candles.

Trap and I blew out the candles as our friends shouted "Happy birthday!"

When the bill arrived, I tried to use my credit card. But it didn't work.

How very, very strange!

"Don't worry, Mr. Stilton. You can pay me next time!" Saucy assured me. I appreciated his kindness, but I was

Yum, yum, yum!

Best wishes, Geronimo!

Happy birthday!

still very embarrassed. A Stilton always pays his debts!

Just then my grandfather William Shortpaws (also known as **Cheap Mouse Willy**) took me aside. "Grandson, why didn't your credit card work? And why did you need three taxis to carry all your packages? And why did you invite everyone you've ever met to the most expensive restaurant in New Mouse City? And

why did you let Trap bring all his friends? Today isn't his birthday – *it's next week, you silly mouse*! He's always playing jokes on you. You've spent a **FORTUNE**! You've turned into a huge spender! Your success has gone straight to your snout! **Now it's up to me to put you in your place!**"

NUTTY'S DREAM

MOULDY MOZZARELLA, what a cheesebrain I'd been!

My mind was racing faster than a gerbil on a wheel. I had to talk this out with Trap.

But my cousin just laughed at me. "Ha, ha, ha! What, you didn't like my little joke, Germeister? What are you complaining about? Now you don't have to worry about shopping for my birthday! Besides, look at how much money I helped you save with all those sales!"

Then he passed me one of the packages (that I had paid for!) and said, "Oh, and by the way, Cousinkins, here you go. Happy birthday!"

He lowered his squeak. "It's seven pairs of pyjamas, one for every day of the week. Take them – I bought the wrong size!"

I took the package and went home feeling glum. What a Cheddarhead I was! I headed straight for bed.

Unfortunately, I still couldn't get those boots off my paws. But I put on the pyjamas that said Saturday anyway.

Suddenly, the doorbell rang.

DING-DONG!

It was **NUTTY CHOCORAT**, a dear friend from my childhood.

"Geronimo, I'm so sorry I didn't make it to your party. I was working on a brand-new project that's

very important, which is what brings me here tonight," he explained.

"Don't worry, Nutty," I assured him. "I'm always here for you if you need me."

"Oh, thank you, Geronimo. I knew I could count on you! Let me explain: you know that I like chocolate ..."

I smiled. Everyone knew how much Nutty *loved* chocolate! "Of course! You are the biggest chocolate expert in New Mouse City."

"Exactly! In fact, I've recently perfected a special formula for new **cheesy chocolates**, and I want to patent the recipe. But I need some start-up money, and I don't have it. Would you be my partner in this new business?"

NUTTY'S SECRET CHOCOLATE STASH

Nutty passed me a cheesy chocolate to try.

"I guess I'll let my taste buds decide," I said, gobbling it up.

31

Yum! I licked my whiskers. **HOLEY CHEESE**, that was the best chocolate I'd ever tasted!

"That chocolate is amazing, Nutty! Of course I'll help you! How much money do you need?"

Nutty told me the amount. It was a lot – enough to buy a lifetime supply of Cheesy Chews!

For a second, I hesitated. But I trusted my friend Nutty and his experience as a **CHOCOLATIER**.

The amount Nutty needed was exactly the amount I always kept in my emergency safe – not a pound more,

It's good, right?

It's marvemouse!

32

not a pound less. I opened the safe and gave him the entire sum. "Use this wisely, Nutty! Patent your – that is, *our* – recipe right away."

Nutty went away happy. "You won't regret this, Geronimo! **It'll be a mouserific success!**"

How much do you need?

THE WORST SUNDAY OF MY LIFE!

What a sleepysnout!

I fed my fish Hannibal …

1 The next day was Sunday. I woke up later than usual. I fixed myself breakfast, checked the paper for the latest news, watered the plants on my balcony, and fed my little red fish Hannibal.

2 I switched on my laptop and went to my bank's website. Yawning, I glanced at how much money was in my account …

Let's see …

I turned on my laptop to check my account …

3 Then I rubbed my eyes and blinked in disbelief.

"WH**AAAAAAAAAAAA**T**TT**? There are zero pounds in my account?! ZERO? Zerooooooo?!"

4 I made it to my favourite pawchair just in time to faint.

There are zero pounds in my account?

I fainted!

When I came to, the first thing I saw was the kind snout of my darling nephew Benjamin. "Uncle G, are you okay?"

I slowly got up. "Yes, thanks, Benjamin! I just had a

nightmare. I dreamed that I had no money in my bank account, but that's impossible ..."

Then my gaze fell on the laptop screen, and I saw that there was indeed no money in my bank account!

This had to be a mistake. I was about to faint again, but before I could, the door swung open, and who should storm in but Grandfather William!

WHAT A NIGHTMARE!

You okay, Uncle G?

"**Geronimo, what happened?**" he boomed.

"Grandfather, what are you doing here?" I cried.

"Uncle Geronimo, I was worried about you, so I called him," Benjamin squeaked.

Grandfather patted his little ears. "Very good, Benjamin. You knew what to do in the case of an emergency! Always call William Shortpaws!

Now, Geronimo, you are paler than a slice of mozzarella. What happened? Tell me ... and make sure it's the truth!"

Uh-oh! The last mouse I wanted to tell about my empty bank account was my grandfather. (There's a reason his nickname is **Cheap Mouse Willy**.) By the time he stopped scolding me, it'd be time for my next birthday!

This had to be the worst Sunday of my life!

Zero? That's Impossible!

Grandfather Shortpaws stared me down like a hungry **CAT**.

"Um, Grandfather, I, er, I checked my bank account, and … well, it would seem … that is, it looks like … but it must be an error!" I sputtered.

Paws quivering, I pointed at the screen. When Grandfather saw that I had no money, his fur **BRISTLED**. He raised his glasses so he could scowl at me freely. "What?! You have zero pounds in your bank account?" he yowled. "You've squandered your life savings? But how? And why?! I've been teaching you to save since you were just a wee mouseling. Why, I started telling you about the value of hard-earned money when you were in your cradle! I gave you a piggy bank shaped like cheese for your fifth birthday. I've been teaching you to save for years! Have you learned nothing from your grandfather?"

"Grandfather, I can't explain it!" I **SOBBED**. "I had thousands in my savings account just a day ago! I don't know how my balance can be zero!" I paused to think for a minute.

"Well, yesterday I did a little shopping with Trap ... There were sales, and I spent all my cash. I used up all my cheques, and then my credit card was declined ..."

"So you admit it! You wasted all your money! You silly **CHEESE PUFF**!" Grandfather barked.

"There must be some mistake," I whispered. "I need

Happy birthday!

Piggy bank my grandfather gave me for my fifth birthday!

Thanks, Grandfather!

to talk to the bank immediately, but today is Sunday, and it's closed till tomorrow ..."

"**Quiet!** Let me think. If you keep on squeaking, I can't concentrate!" Grandfather declared. "Hmm, hmmm, hmmmm ..."

Then he grabbed his phone and called someone.

I couldn't tell who he was squeaking with, although I did hear him grumble, "My wasteful grandson needs to learn a lesson, one he'll never forget! ... Yes, a lesson on saving ... Must be made to learn the value of money ... You think about it, since you are the experts ... Yes, I knew I could count on you!"

He hung up the phone and glared at me. "I suppose now you want to ask me for help."

"Um, yes," I admitted.

"I will help you, Geronimo, but you must do as I say, understand?" Grandfather thundered.

I hung my snout in shame. But I had no choice. I needed his help!

"Yes, Grandfather. I'll do whatever you tell me."

Grandfather grabbed me by the ear. "Good! Now you will leave immediately for a CRASH COURSE in saving!"

"But, Grandfather ..." I began to protest.

"No 'buts'!" he shouted. "You must leave immediately! I've arranged it all for you. If you don't learn fast, we'll be forced to sell The Rodent's Gazette to pay your debts!"

"Sell *The Rodent's Gazette*? Never!" I yelled desperately.

"Yes, we can sell it to Sally Ratmousen. I'm sure she'd be interested," Grandfather replied, stroking his whiskers thoughtfully.

I pictured Sally Ratmousen, who runs *The Daily Rat*. She was my number one competitor … and my nemesis! She'd tap her pink polished pawnails on my telephone, put her paws up on my desk, and boss around my staff, threatening to fire them every five minutes. **NEVER!**

"Come along now, Grandson. You're lucky I'm here to whip your finances into shape!" Grandfather scolded me.

"Okay, but where am I going?" I asked.

"There's only one rodent who can help you now: SAMUEL S. STINGYSNOUT!"

I turned paler than a slice of Swiss cheese. Samuel S. Stingysnout is my uncle. He also happens to be the **stingiest** rodent on Mouse Island!

Grandfather William passed me his mobile phone. **"Here, call Uncle Samuel and squeak to him yourself!"**

THE STINGYSNOUT FAMILY

The Stingysnouts come from the Valley of Lack. For many years, they lived at Penny-Pincher Castle, their ancestral family home. Now they have relocated to Mouldy Manor in the Valley of Thrift.

UNCLE SAMUEL S. STINGYSNOUT

Head of the Stingysnout family. He's always devising new ways to save!

STEVIE STINGYSNOUT

Samuel's son. When he combs his whiskers, he saves the ones that fall out and uses them as dental floss!

CHINTZINA STILTON (NÉE STINGYSNOUT)

Samuel's younger sister. She is less stingy now that she has married a Stilton!

ZELDA STINGYSNOUT

Stevie's cousin. She's so stingy, she wears steel heels on her shoes so they never wear out!

The relationship between the Stingysnouts and the Stiltons goes back many generations, to the time when Samuel's great-grandfather married Geronimo's great-great-grandmother. Like the Stiltons, the Stingysnouts are very good-hearted. Unlike the Stiltons, they are very stingy!

THRIFTELLA and WORTHINGTON

Twins who save money by always wearing the same clothes!

GRANDMA and GRANDPA CHEAPERLY

Samuel's parents. They taught their children everything they know about penny-pinching!

IVY and HOARDEN ACCOUNTS

Samuel's daughter and her husband. She saves calories by eating fat-free cheese; he saves money on heat by wearing three pairs of thermals at a time!

PENNIFORD and SAVEANNA

Children of Hoarden and Ivy. They make their Cheddar pops last for years by taking just one lick a month!

MOULDY MANOR

I gave up and said hello to Uncle Stingysnout.

"NEPHEW!" he sighed in a tragic tone. "How ever did you get yourself into this mess? You've wasted all your money. What an embarrassment for the family! How could you? Oh, Nephew, this is just *terrible*. But don't worry. I'll set you back on the narrow road of responsibility! You will learn to save, even if it takes the whole Stingysnout family to teach you! That's what family is for, right? By the time we're done with you, you'll be saving money like a **stingy little squirrel!** So listen up, and I'll explain how to get to Mouldy Manor."

I was astonished. "MOULDY MANOR? But doesn't the Stingysnout family live at Penny-Pincher Castle?"

"No, no, we are all at Mouldy Manor now. After

we fixed up Penny-Pincher Castle, we had to move. That place was getting *too fancy!*" Uncle Samuel snorted. "Here, let me give you directions. First, you head towards the VALLEY OF THRIFT. Then turn down Lack Lane and cross over Mount Stingy. Take the turn for Lake Cheapskate. Once you pass Pinchpenny River, you'll arrive at Thrifty City. Look for Tightwad Turnpike. Turn right at Squirrel Street, and you'll find yourself at Scrooge Alley. Mouldy Manor is number thirteen. **I'll be expecting you!**"

I hung up. I was already dreading the trip, but I had to go to Mouldy Manor if I wanted to save The Rodent's Gazette. I didn't have a choice!

My sister Thea scurried in. "Geronimo, what happened? Your bank account is at zero? Didn't you keep track of how much you spent?"

"Um, y-yes," I stammered. "Well, actually, no. Trap threw away all my receipts ..."

"Here, I brought you something," said Thea, passing

VALLEY OF THRIFT

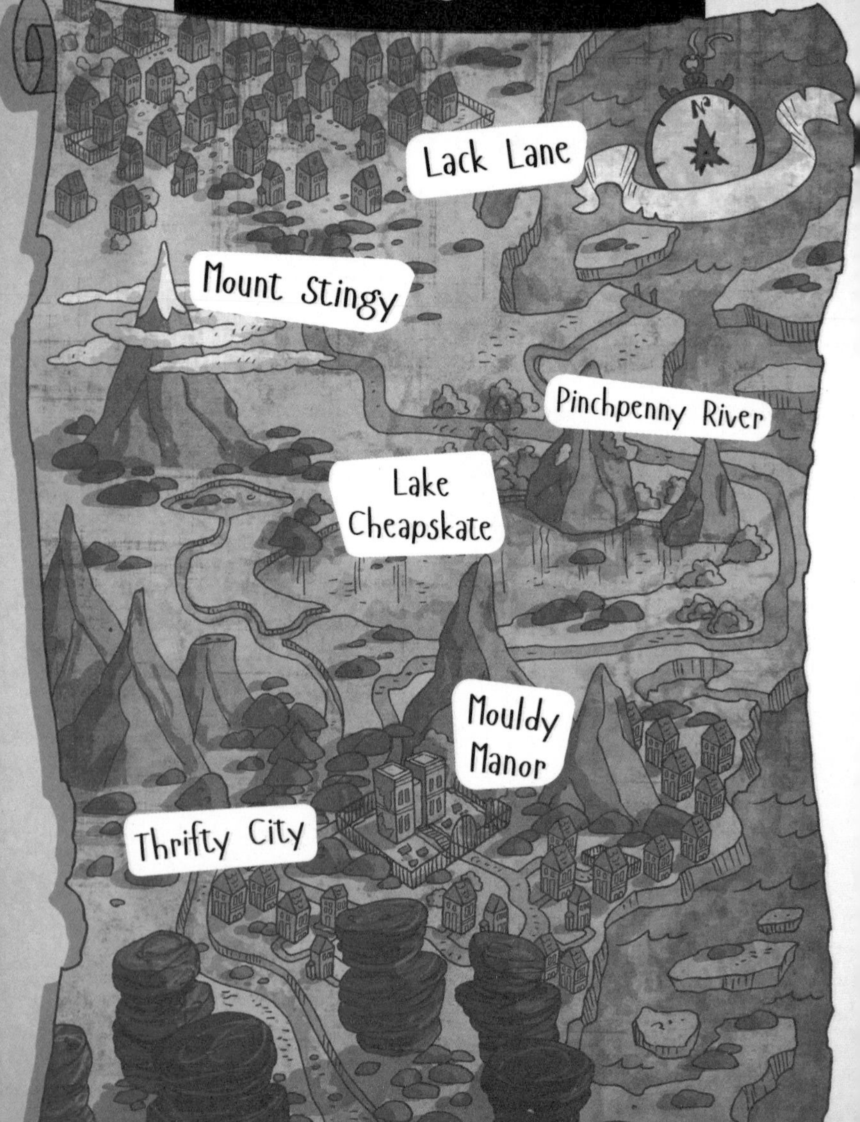

me a red notebook. "Use it to write down everything you spend. I've been doing it for a while. It's a good habit to get into, and it's very useful for keeping your money situation under control."

As my sister finished squeaking, Benjamin passed me his piggy bank. "Don't worry, Uncle G! Here's my **piggy bank.** I want you to have all my savings!"

I felt my tail sag with embarrassment. I wanted to be a role model for Benjamin, and now my little nephew was looking out for me instead!

Trap had followed Thea in.

"**GERMEISTER**, what a stew you've gotten yourself into! Now who's going to take me on holiday? Who will

LEARN TO KEEP TRACK OF ALL THE MONEY THAT YOU EARN AND SPEND IN A LITTLE NOTEBOOK. IT'S A GOOD HABIT!

pay for my birthday parties now, huh?" He sighed. "But don't worry, Gerry, we still love you. **Take this token of my affection and generosity**."

He opened his paw and gave me a brown jacket button.

"A brown button?" I said uncertainly. "But all my jackets are green!"

A brown button?!

Trap snorted. "At this point, you have nothing, Cousinkins! Are you really turning up your snout at my gift? Take it and say thank you!"

My fur turned redder than a cheese rind. Trap was right. I had nothing!

Time to go ...

I thanked him and scurried upstairs to throw a few things in my suitcase. Then I left for MOULDY MANOR.

WELCOME TO MOULDY MANOR!

Grandfather had made all my travel arrangements at a steep discount! So instead of a half-hour direct flight to Mouldy Manor, it took me:

1 **THREE HOURS** in a third-class train compartment

2  **SIX HOURS** by bus

Yikes!

3 **THIRTY MILES** by bike – but I got a puncture, so I had to ride the rest of the way in a cart full of manure! **4**

I had to travel the last mile by paw, and my new boots were pinching my toes like crazy!

It was sunset by the time I arrived at Mouldy Manor. Though it was getting dark, all the lights were off.

The manor was a large building the colour of **STALE CHEESE**. I could tell it hadn't been painted in ages (to save money, naturally!). There were broken bricks and boards everywhere. Parts of the manor seemed unsafe. Uncle Samuel had posted signs that said things like Go around the balconies, they may collapse; Go around the gutters or they'll fall on your snout; and Go around, or just go away!

There were other signs, too: We don't buy anything! and Absolutely no loans, especially not to friends and family!

I looked around in the dark for a doorbell, but all I found was another sign: No doorbell (to save money fixing it). Go ahead and yell; you'll only waste your own breath!

"Is anyone home?" I shouted.

The curtains in a first-floor window twitched. A snout with long whiskers peeked out at me. It was Uncle Samuel!

"Who is it? Who's bothering me? No salesmice, please. We won't buy anything!"

"It's me, Uncle Samuel! It's your nephew Geronimo!"

"Is that you, Geronimo?" Uncle Samuel said, squinting.

"Yes, it's me. **Why is everything so dark?**"

"Nephew, you have so much to learn," Uncle Samuel sighed. "It's to save money, naturally!"

I scurried to the door, but I noticed writing on the doormat: Don't wipe your paws on the doormat. You'll wear it out!

I opened the door and spotted another message: take off your shoes, or you'll wear out the floor! I let out a low moan. I really, really wanted to take off my boots, but they were stuck to my paws like a **GLUE TRAP**!

I closed the door and stepped inside. It was so dark that I banged my snout against a column and gave myself a black eye!

"**YEE-OUCH!**" I shouted.

I tried to turn on the lights, but an antique chandelier fell right on top of me, scraping my ear!

"*OWWW!*" I howled.

As I hopped up and down in pain, a floorboard popped up and slammed down on my tail!

"*OUCH OUCH OUCHIE!*"

Uncle Samuel strode in holding a candle stump. "Nephew, don't yell like that. You'll wear out your vocal cords!" he scolded me. *"We can't spare the money to buy you medicine for a sore throat!"*

57

THIS ROOM FOR PAYING GUESTS ONLY!

Uncle Samuel's son Stevie followed him into the room. Stevie was a tall, thin rodent with a patched jacket. Behind him were Grandma and Grandpa Cheaperly, who were shaking their snouts at me sadly. **"So you've turned into a big spender, eh, Geronimo?"**

The Stingysnouts escorted me to my room. A strange sign hung on the door: This room for paying guests only! I pushed open the squeaky door. In the candlelight, I saw an ancient, **BROKEN-DOWN** canopy bed.

I tried to close the curtain, which smelled of mould, but the canopy fell on my snout and left a big bump!

Next I tried to sit on a chair, but it had been chewed by **termites** and collapsed under me. When I tried to put it back together, I got a splinter in my paw!

Then I tried to lie down on the mattress, but there

was a spring sticking out, and it poked me in the tail! **OOOOOWWWW!**

As I was **checking** the bump on my snout, **examining** my wounded paw, and **massaging** my tail, Uncle Samuel approached me with his paw outstretched. "Okay, Nephew, time to pay up!"

I was astonished. **"Wh-what? I thought I was your guest!"**

"Didn't you see the sign on the door? This room is for paying guests only. You must pay for your stay. So give me the dough! This is your first lesson, Nephew: *if you want to save money, never give anything away for free!*"

Why, that wasn't saving money, **it was stinginess!** But I wasn't in a position to protest.

"Uncle, you know very well that I don't have any money," I replied.

Uncle Samuel sighed. "All right, because you're family, I'll let you barter. In return for the room, you can give me your **NICE GOLD WATCH**."

Dear reader, I really didn't want to pass him that watch. My sister Thea gave it to me years ago, and I loved it dearly. But I had to stay at Mouldy Manor to complete my crash course and save The Rodent's Gazette!

Uncle Samuel snatched

GERONIMO'S WATCH, A GIFT FROM THEA

61

the watch out of my paws. Then he turned tail and left. "Good night, Nephew! Try not to dream too much – you need to save your energy!"

Once he was gone, I realised there were **TEARS** in my eyes. I was alone and desperate. I missed my cosy house; my super-comfy room; my super-full refrigerator; my little red fish Hannibal; my family; and most of all, **my darling nephew Benjamin**.

I decided to call him, but I couldn't get a signal on my mobile phone. Weird!

Instead, I thought I would take a hot shower. I needed it after that ride in the manure cart!

I lathered up my fur and turned on the tap. A jet of ice-cold water sprayed me in the snout. That's when I noticed another sign: Insert coins for hot water. Otherwise, cold water only!

I didn't know what to do. Would I rather rinse off with cold water or have soapy fur?

I didn't want to catch a **cold**, so I decided to keep my fur sudsy. **1** But my boots were already filled with **freezing** water, and there was an **icy** draught blowing from a broken window. **2** So I caught a **chill**, anyway! **3** The sheets reeked of mould. I put a clothes peg on my snout so I wouldn't suffocate from the stench. **4** The one thin blanket was infested with fleas. **5** Soon, I had bites all over ... and my boots were still SOAKED with water, which made it impossible to sleep. **6**

What an unbearable night at Mouldy Manor!

WHAT A **NIGHT** AT MOULDY MANOR!

1 Since I didn't want to rinse off with cold water, I stayed soapy.

2 Icy draughts were gusting through the broken window.

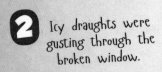

3 I got a terrible cold and sneezed all night long.

A Stingy Breakfast

The next morning, I got up early and headed down to the kitchen.

Uncle Samuel was there to greet me. "Nephew, eat some breakfast so you'll have energy for our crash course in saving."

My fur went whiter than a mozzarella ball when I saw what was on the kitchen table. There was only:

1 DROP of milk in a thimble,

1 SLIVER of banana on a bottle cap (so we wouldn't have to wash a plate!),

1 PIECE of broken biscuit on **1 SQUARE** of toilet paper (to save a napkin!)

"Geronimo, dear, don't forget you must pay for breakfast. Since you have no money, you can give me your waistcoat instead."

"But, Uncle ..." I protested.

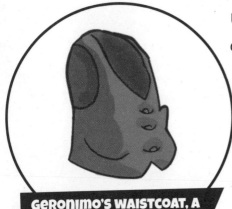

GERONIMO'S WAISTCOAT, A GIFT FROM AUNT SWEETFUR

Uncle Samuel patted me on the tail. "If you want to eat, fork over the waistcoat, Nephew!"

This time, I refused. My waistcoat was a gift from Aunt Sweetfur, and I wasn't about to give it up for such a minuscule meal. Even if I ate it, I'd still be starving!

Uncle Samuel didn't back down. "Very well, dear Nephew ... today we will begin your personal crash course in saving. Your instructor is the greatest expert on saving money in the VALLEY OF THRIFT. He just happens to be my third cousin, twice removed – the very famous Miserly Parsimouse. He's nicknamed the **Wallet Watchrat** because when it's time to pay the bill, he automatically hides his wallet."

As Uncle Samuel was squeaking, the door flung open, and a rodent with GREY FUR strode in.

He had on a worn-out grey jacket with a fake collar and cuffs sewn on (to save him from having to wear a dress shirt!).

Miserly's SHINY grey trousers were a masterpiece of patchwork. He had a fake tie complete with a fake tiepin – it was stitched right on the collar of his shirt (also fake!). I could tell that he washed himself with cold water instead of soap because he gave off the distinct odour of old cheese.

"**I AM MISERLY PARSIMOUSE**, also called the Wallet Watchrat, and proud of it! I'm the

I am Miserly Parsimouse!

greatest expert on saving money in the Valley of Thrift. I even wrote a book on the subject … Look!"

He placed a **MASSIVE BOOK** in my paws.

"To prepare for the crash course in saving, you must study my textbook, *Saving Money from A to Z*. I've patented this method! I was inspired by the teachings of my ancestor Augustus 'Greedy Gus' Parsimouse. Now, there was a mouse who knew how to save. Compared to him, I am an amateur!"

Uncle Samuel was moved. "Learn from this mouse, Nephew! Take inspiration from him! Imitate him!" He dried a tear on my tie. "Can I use your tie as a tissue? I don't use tissues because I don't like to waste them!"

"Excuse me, Geronimo. My book is EXPENSIVE," Miserly coughed. "But your uncle told me you don't have any money. If you want, I will accept your **GOLD PEN** as payment …"

I took off my

GERONIMO'S GOLD PEN, A GIFT FROM GRANDFATHER WILLIAM

glasses so I could cry freely. I was so fond of that pen! But I gave it to Miserly. I had no choice!

Miserly passed me the book. "And now **study, study, study!** You must learn this textbook by heart. Once you've mastered the theory, we will move on to its application!"

And so I began reading the course description and Miserly Parsimouse's biography ...

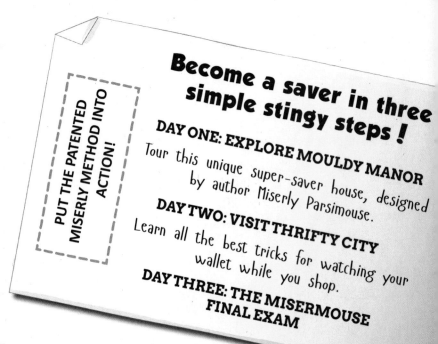

PUT THE PATENTED MISERLY METHOD INTO ACTION!

Become a saver in three simple stingy steps !

DAY ONE: EXPLORE MOULDY MANOR

Tour this unique super-saver house, designed by author Miserly Parsimouse.

DAY TWO: VISIT THRIFTY CITY

Learn all the best tricks for watching your wallet while you shop.

DAY THREE: THE MISERMOUSE FINAL EXAM

MISERLY PARSIMOUSE

MISERLY PARSIMOUSE, nicknamed the **WALLET WATCHRAT** for his stinginess, is the biggest expert on saving money in the **VALLEY OF THRIFT**. He graduated from Cheaprat College at the top of his class, majoring in stinginess and saving. Parsimouse's manual **SAVING MONEY FROM A TO Z** became an instant bestseller.

Miserly has trained nearly all the rodents in the Valley of Thrift in his crash course "**BECOME A SAVER IN THREE SIMPLE STINGY STEPS**". The Miserly method is guaranteed! There isn't a rodent who hasn't become more economical (even downright cheap!) after following his simple approach to saving money.

Day One: A Thrifty House

My crash course began at 10 a.m. sharp.

Miserly called me into Mouldy Manor's grimy study, where no one ever dusted – Uncle Samuel didn't want to waste the FEATHERS in the feather duster!

"Okay, big spender, over the next three days, I'll take your extravagant ideas on spending and transform them into ways to save! Stick with me, and you'll become a thrifty mouse. You have the word of Miserly Parsimouse, the **Number One Saver in Thrifty City!**"

Sigh!

I was **a little glum** about getting a personalised crash course from Miserly. Was I so hopeless that I needed help from Mouse Island's greatest expert? Sighing, I began to take notes.

"Our first lesson will be how to run a thrifty house," Miserly squeaked. "Tomorrow, you'll visit Thrifty City so that you can learn to resist the temptation to shop. On our third and final day, you'll take my FINAL EXAM."

I knew these next three days would be unbearable. But I had to make Grandfather happy. And I absolutely had to hold on to The Rodent's Gazette! So I just nodded and held my tongue.

Miserly pulled out a crumpled old cheese wrapper and wrote Geronimo's Report Card across the top. "I will give you a plus for each question you answer correctly, and a minus for each one you answer incorrectly!" he said solemnly.

Miserly began listing his favourite tricks for saving money. "Let's start with the kitchen. First, put a padlock on your pantry. That way, you won't be able to eat too much, and you'll save a bundle on food. Also, the less

74

you clean, the better off you are. You'll save on rags, and you won't scratch the furniture. Plus, you won't exert yourself, so you won't need to eat as much, which will save money on food! And you won't **SWEAT**, so you won't waste water washing yourself, and you won't need to change your clothes!"

Miserly grinned at me. "The ideal would be to learn to not breathe, so you don't **WASTE AIR**, but no one has ever figured out a way to do that. My great-great-grandfather tried, but he died during the course of the experiment, poor rodent!"

We went into the living room, where the furniture was still covered with 𝐏𝐥𝐚𝐬𝐭𝐢𝐜 like it had been the day it was delivered.

Miserly pointed at the chairs and couches proudly. "See? Your uncle never unwrapped them, so they won't

Thrifty Living Room

COLLECTION OF ANTIQUE PIGGY BANKS!

PAINTED FLAMES

FURNITURE STILL COVERED IN PLASTIC!

PATCHED RUG!

be damaged! What a brilliant way to save!"

In the fireplace, there were flames, but it was so cold in the room, I realised they were painted on.

"Are the flames painted on to save wood?" I asked Miserly.

Miserly marked a plus on my report card. "**Very good!** See, you're already beginning to catch on."

We headed for the bathroom. "Remember: don't use energy and you won't sweat, and then you won't have to wash yourself," Miserly advised me.

Then it was time for the bedroom. Miserly kept me there for hours, explaining all the secrets to saving.

We finished the lesson in the hallway, where he showed me the wallpaper. It was made of paper scraps glued to the wall ... to save money, obviously!

At the end of the day, Miserly said goodbye. "**Sleep well, Geronimo!** Tomorrow we'll be busy with your tour of Thrifty City."

Despite all the energy I'd saved, I was exhausted!

I was also starving. I ran to the kitchen, where Uncle

Thrifty Bedroom

VINTAGE ANTI-DRAUGHT COBWEBS

NO HEAT!

LOCKS TO AVOID WEARING NEW CLOTHES

PATCHED SHEET – NO NEED TO WASH IT!

Samuel was waiting for me. "Ah, Nephew, you're too late! Dinner has already been served, and there's nothing left over. I'm sorry, but you simply must get here earlier."

"But I was at my lesson!" I protested.

"Okay, I'll prepare my specialty for you: The very tasty Stingysnout Special … in exchange for your nice red belt!"

This time, I couldn't refuse. I was hungrier than a rodent on a Mousefast diet. I chomped on a teeny-

GERONIMO'S BELT, A GIFT FROM TRAP

tiny sandwich: two slices of **STALE BREAD** with a crust of cheese and a drop of **RANCID** mayonnaise, topped with a sliver of **MOULDY** cucumber.

"By the way, did you squeak to Benjamin?" Uncle Samuel asked. "He phoned earlier

79

and said he wanted to squeak to you, but he didn't say why."

The thought of Benjamin **cheered** me up. "Oh, great! I'll call him back now."

Uncle Samuel pointed at the ancient phone hanging on the wall. "Oh, sorry, this telephone only receives calls – you can't call out from here. And don't bother trying to use your mobile phone. There's no service!"

I let out a deep sigh. Well, at least I'd save money on my phone bill!

There was nothing left to do but go to bed. At least I didn't have to take another cold shower – with all the energy I'd saved, **there was no need to wash!**

GERONIMO'S MOBILE PHONE

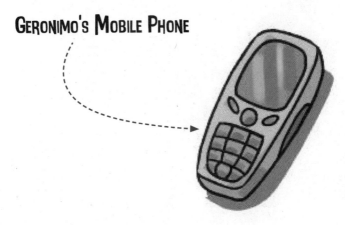

Day Two: Thrifty City

At breakfast the next day, I was **RAVENOUS**. For a fee, Uncle Samuel prepared me a slice of toast spread with a light layer of cream cheese. I devoured it. After I finished, I even picked up all the crumbs off the table and ate them!

Uncle Samuel approved. "Well done, Nephew. See, you've already learned not to waste a single **crumb**!"

In exchange for the toast, he made me give him my jacket.

That day was reserved for a tour of **THRIFTY CITY**, the capital of the Valley of Thrift. Miserly came to get me — on paw, naturally, so as not to waste petrol. I would have

GERONIMO'S JACKET, A PRESENT FROM AUNT SUGARFUR

preferred not to walk, since the green boots were pinching my toes more than ever, but I didn't want to waste any energy protesting!

When we arrived in Spendthrift Square, the centre of Thrifty City, I looked around curiously. The signs on all the stores were off.

"What time do the stores open here?" I asked Miserly.

Miserly shook his snout. "What a waste of a **BREATH** that question is, Stilton! The stores are already open, but the signs are obviously turned off to save money!" He marked a minus on my report card.

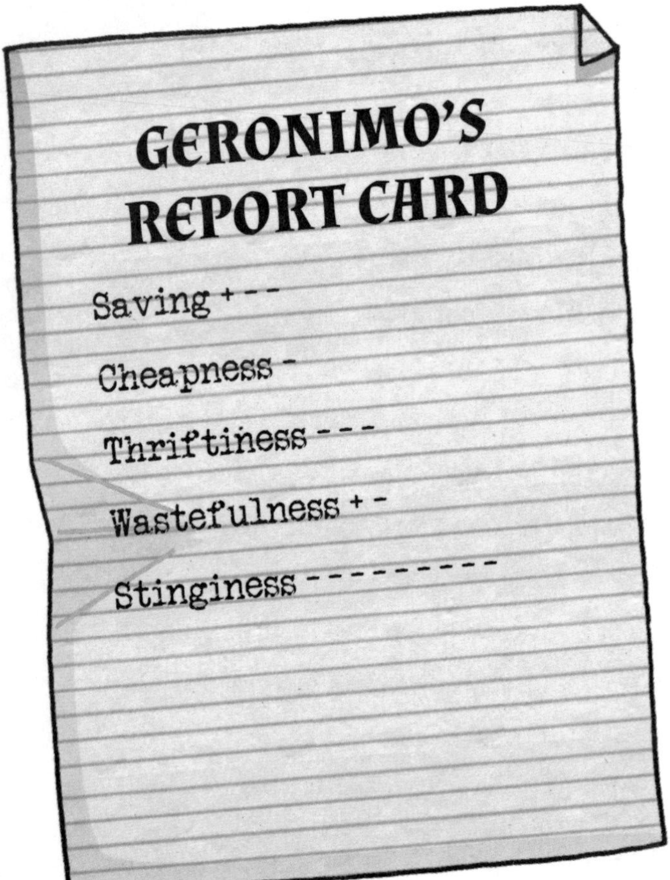

GERONIMO'S REPORT CARD

Saving + - -

Cheapness -

Thriftiness - - -

Wastefulness + -

Stinginess - - - - - - - - -

I smacked myself on the snout. What a cheesebrain I was! I should have known why the signs were all off: to save ELECTRICITY, of course!

I spotted a rodent pushing a motorcycle with the engine turned off. Thinking it was broken, I went over to help him.

The rodent was offended. "Mister, has the cheese slipped off your cracker? There's nothing wrong with my motorcycle. I'm just pushing it to save gas, naturally!"

Miserly marked another minus on my report card. But this time, he didn't bother saying a thing – to save his breath!

What a **SillySnout** I was! I was trying my hardest, but I couldn't be as stingy as Miserly and Uncle Samuel. It just wasn't in me!

I began to get very thirsty. That toast spread with cream cheese was going up and down in my stomach like a ROLLER COASTER at Mousey World. I needed to drink something, but I knew better than to ask Miserly to buy water. I didn't want any more minuses on my report card!

I looked around for a water fountain, but there wasn't one. That's when I saw a bicycle with **IRON WHEELS** pass by.

IRON WHEELS

Miserly sighed. Predicting my question, he said, "The wheels are made of iron to avoid wearing out the rubber tyres, naturally!"

By now, I was parched. When I saw a fountain, I dashed over to get a drink, but ... **SURPRISE!** In Thrifty City, even the public water fountains have a fee.

"How much does it cost?" I asked Miserly.

"Too much! Wait till we're back at Mouldy Manor, Geronimo," he replied.

COIN-OPERATED
FOUNTAIN

I was terribly **thirsty**, but Miserly led me away by the paw, saying, "Enough wasting time! Now we'll begin a new lesson on how to resist the temptation of shopping. After today, you won't be a big spender anymore. You have the MISERLY GUARANTEE!"

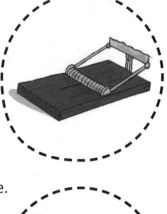

As we scampered along Main Street, I spotted many signs for sales. To help me resist the temptation, Miserly put a mousetrap in my wallet. He made me wear special mittens with a padlock on the wrists so I wouldn't be able to sign any cheques.

Then he gave me a MousePod with headphones. I

was hoping for some relaxing music, but it turned out to be Miserly's squeak repeating the words, *"Friends don't let friends spend!"*

Finally, he made me put on dark glasses so I wouldn't be lured into shops. Unfortunately, the glasses were so dark I couldn't see a thing ... and scampered straight into a lamp post!

OUCHIE! That hurt!

I CAN'T SEE A THING!

OOF! MY SNOUT!

Day Three: The Misermouse Final Exam

At the end of the day, I was zonked. But that night, I never closed my eyes. Between the fleas biting my fur and the boots pinching my paws, I was in agony!

The next morning, my eyelids were heavier than a pound of **PETRIFIED PARMESAN**. I could hardly move. But I reminded myself it was the last day. I could take the test, and then I could go home.

I dragged my sorry tail into the living room of Mouldy Manor. Miserly was there waiting for me. Solemnly, he passed me the **MISERMOUSE FINAL EXAM**. "I recommend you answer these questions honestly, Geronimo!" he advised me.

I sat at the desk and began to read the test. Holey

cheese, if I answered honestly, I'd never pass it! I swear on a block of Cheddar, I am not now, nor will I ever be,

a penny-pincher!

I couldn't bring myself to lie. I just couldn't fake it!

When I'd finished, I passed my paper back to Miserly. "I'm sorry, but I don't think I passed the test." I sighed. "I can't pretend to be stingy. I like to share what I have with my friends, and now that I have less, it just means that I will have less to share.

I will never be stingy!

THE MISERMOUSE FINAL EXAM

1. IT'S THE BIRTHDAY OF YOUR SECOND COUSIN, ONCE REMOVED. YOU ...

A. Buy her very expensive cheesy chocolates.

B. Send a box of chocolates you've already opened, but you wrap it nicely.

C. Send an affectionate birthday card.

D. Pretend you forgot, just like last year.

2. WHEN YOU'RE HEADING TO WORK, YOU ...

A. Drive yourself. Petrol is expensive, but driving is comfortable and easy.

B. Take the subway.

C. Walk. That's the healthy way.

D. Make your friend come pick you up – it's cheaper that way.

3. HOW OFTEN DO YOU BORROW YOUR NEIGHBOUR'S BICYCLE?

A. Never

B. Occasionally

C. About once a week

D. So often that my neighbour has to borrow it back from me!

4. YOU NEED TO MAKE A PHONE CALL. YOU …

A. Grab your mobile phone and start dialling.

B. Wait till you're home, then call from a landline.

C. Make the call short, using as few minutes as possible.

D. Stop someone on the street and ask to borrow his phone, saying it's an emergency!

5. WHEN YOU'RE ON HOLIDAY, YOU …

A. Don't care what you spend.

B. Choose the place that has the best quality for the best price.

C. Spend as little money as possible on transportation and hotel.

D. Tag along on a friend's holiday. Isn't that what friends are for?

6. YOU ARE INVITED TO A BLACK-TIE PARTY. YOU …

A. Buy a very expensive designer tuxedo.

B. Rent a nice-looking tuxedo.

C. Borrow a tuxedo from your cousin who's a foot shorter than you. It's better than nothing, and it's free!

D. Have a new tuxedo hanging in your closet, but you go in jogging bottoms. You don't want to ruin your new tux!

7. YOU WANT TO IMPRESS A RODENT YOU'VE JUST MET. YOU …

A. Send her two dozen red roses.

B. Bring her a bouquet of flowers you bought at the supermarket.

C. Visit the cemetery — there are always free flowers there!

D. Invite her out to dinner and make her pay!

ANSWER KEY: A TRUE MISERMOUSE ALWAYS PICKS D!

"Miserly, I want to thank you," I continued. "Your crash course really taught me how to save money, even if it's more of a course on stinginess than on saving!"

Miserly's snout was filled with emotion. He dried a tear and wiped his snout on my tie (to avoid wasting tissues, of course).

"Sniff ... **that was beautiful, Geronimo!** I am moved," he said. "Although we are very different, and you are a shameless squanderer, I've come to respect you."

Thanks from the bottom of my heart!

Sniff sniff!

I shook his paw. "I respect you, too. Thank you for everything you've taught me."

Miserly squeezed my paw. "How wonderful! Now we're the best of friends! But you still need to pay for the crash course. I never give credit, especially not to my friends."

"Um, I would like to pay you, but I really don't know how I can ..." I said.

He raised an eyebrow and pointed to my boots. "What about those?"

I shrugged. "It's a deal. If you can get them off, they're all yours!"

Miserly soon realised he'd got more than he'd bargained for. He called in the whole Stingysnout family to help. Together, they began to pull … and pull … and pull … Suddenly, there was a loud pop, and my paws were free at last!

THANK GOODMOUSE! What a relief! And pee-yoo, what stinky paws!

It was time to say goodbye. I really wanted to know

the results of the test, but Miserly said he'd promised to tell Grandfather first.

I scurried home to my **snug little mousehole**. I was weary, worn, wiped out ... and absolutely *starving!*

In the fridge, I had nothing but leftover cheese rinds. They seemed a little hard, but I ate them, anyway. They couldn't be worse than the meals at Mouldy Manor.

How delicious they tasted!

How soft my bed felt!

And how cosy my house was!

But despite all the comforts of home, I was still stressed about my score on the test.

Bad News ... and Good News!

The next morning, my doorbell **RANG** early. It was Benjamin and Grandfather Shortpaws! I was thrilled to see them.

"Grandson, how was the crash course in saving?" Grandfather demanded.

"It wasn't a crash course in saving; it was an advanced course in stinginess!" I replied. "It was terrible. I only

How was the course?

ACK!

stayed because my bank account is at zero and I didn't want to lose The Rodent's Gazette. So, tell me, how did I do on the test?"

My whiskers **trembled** with anxiety as I waited for Grandfather's answer.

"Er, well, Grandson, I have bad news and good news," Grandfather said.

I had a feeling my grandfather was nervous. But why? Grandfather never got nervous about anything!

"Look, Geronimo, let me – what I need to tell you is ..." he stammered. Then he took a deep breath. "The bad news is you didn't pass the test."

I tore at my fur. "Oh no! I've lost The Rodent's Gazette!" I cried.

Grandfather cut me off before I could squeak another word. "But the good news is that you have more than zero pounds in your bank account!"

"What?!" I shrieked. "But I saw the balance with my own two eyes! My account was down to zero!"

Grandfather snorted. "Geronimo, your account showed a balance of zero on Sunday morning. But on

Monday your bank called to say there was an error. You actually still had money in your account!"

I sighed with relief. "So everything is okay! Why didn't you tell me right away?"

"I called you, but you didn't answer the phone, and at Mouldy Manor, you can't call back," Benjamin squeaked.

"Well, Grandson, I hope you're not going to complain," Grandfather said. "The crash course was good for you. In the future, you should think twice before you spend!"

It was true: the course had been good for me. I would never become stingy, but the class had helped me understand the importance of saving – so that I'd have more to share with others!

Just then the telephone rang.

RIIIING, RIIIIIIING, RIIIIIIIING!

"Hello, this is Geronimo Stilton!" I said, picking it up.

It was my dear friend **NUTTY CHOCORAT**. "Hi, Geronimo!" he cried enthusiastically. "While you were away, I opened our store, Chocorat's Choco-Rama. It's been a smash success! Our **cheesy chocolates** have sold out, and we've made a fortune!"

IT WAS A SMASH SUCCESS!

How fabumouse! I passed on the news, and my grandfather congratulated me.

"Grandson, I must admit you were right to make that investment,"

102

he said grumpily. "I knew the store would do well. In business, you must take risks to succeed. You took a risk, and it paid off. Well done!"

To celebrate, I invited the whole family and all my friends to Nutty's new chocolate shop. I even asked Trap along, although he was the one who made this mess and then left me alone to flail like a fly in **FONDUE**! But I can never stay mad at my cousin for long.

I also invited all the Stingysnouts, who eagerly accepted (only because it was free, of course!).

Nutty had dozens of chocolates to sample, and everyone crowded around to try them. Yum!

And so this strange adventure ends as happily as it began. I thought I'd lost everything, but instead I learned a lot and made a new friend. I discovered the art of saving, but also the importance of staying true to myself.

See you next time, dear reader! Till then, I'll be surrounded by my loved ones, **chewing on the finest chocolates on Mouse Island!**

THE RODENT'S GAZETTE

1. Main entrance
2. Printing presses (where everything is printed)
3. Accounts department
4. Editorial room (where editors, illustrators, and designers work)
5. Geronimo Stilton's office
6. Geronimo's botanical garden

MAP OF NEW MOUSE CITY

1. Industrial Zone
2. Cheese Factories
3. Angorat International Airport
4. WRAT Radio and Television Station
5. Cheese Market
6. Fish Market
7. Town Hall
8. Snotnose Castle
9. The Seven Hills of Mouse Island
10. Mouse Central Station
11. Trade Centre
12. Movie Theatre
13. Gym
14. Catnegie Hall
15. Singing Stone Plaza
16. The Gouda Theatre
17. Grand Hotel
18. Mouse General Hospital
19. Botanical Gardens
20. Cheap Junk for Less (Trap's store)
21. Parking Lot
22. Mouseum of Modern Art
23. University and Library
24. The Daily Rat
25. The Rodent's Gazette
26. Trap's House
27. Fashion District
28. The Mouse House Restaurant
29. Environmental Protection Centre
30. Harbour Office
31. Mousidon Square Garden
32. Golf Course
33. Swimming Pool
34. Blushing Meadow Tennis Courts
35. Curlyfur Island Amusement Park
36. Geronimo's House
37. Historic District
38. Public Library
39. Shipyard
40. Thea's House
41. New Mouse Harbour
42. Luna Lighthouse
43. The Statue of Liberty
44. Hercule Poirat's Office
45. Petunia Pretty Paws's House
46. Grandfather William's House

MAP OF MOUSE ISLAND

1. Big Ice Lake
2. Frozen Fur Peak
3. Slipperyslopes Glacier
4. Coldcreeps Peak
5. Ratzikistan
6. Transratania
7. Mount Vamp
8. Roastedrat Volcano
9. Brimstone Lake
10. Poopedcat Pass
11. Stinko Peak
12. Dark Forest
13. Vain Vampires Valley
14. Goosebumps Gorge
15. The Shadow Line Pass
16. Penny-Pincher Castle
17. Nature Reserve Park
18. Las Ratayas Marinas
19. Fossil Forest
20. Lake Lake
21. Lake Lakelake
22. Lake Lakelakelake
23. Cheddar Crag
24. Cannycat Castle
25. Valley of the Giant Sequoia
26. Cheddar Springs
27. Sulphurous Swamp
28. Old Reliable Geyser
29. Vole Vale
30. Ravingrat Ravine
31. Gnat Marshes
32. Munster Highlands
33. Mousehara Desert
34. Oasis of the Sweaty Camel
35. Cabbagehead Hill
36. Rattytrap Jungle
37. Rio Mosquito
38. Mousefort Beach
39. San Mouscisco
40. Swissville
41. Cheddarton
42. Mouseport
43. New Mouse City
44. Pirate Ship of Cats

HAVE YOU READ ALL OF GERONIMO'S ADVENTURES?

ABOUT THE AUTHOR

Born in New Mouse City, Mouse Island, GERONIMO STILTON is Rattus Emeritus of Mousomorphic Literature and of Neo-Ratonic Comparative Philosophy. For the past twenty years, he has been running The Rodent's Gazette, New Mouse City's most widely read daily newspaper.

Stilton was awarded the Ratitzer Prize for his scoops on *The Curse of the Cheese Pyramid* and *The Search for Sunken Treasure*. He has also received the Andersen Prize

for Personality of the Year. His works have been published all over the globe.

In his spare time, Mr. Stilton collects antique cheese rinds and plays golf. But what he most enjoys is telling stories to his nephew Benjamin.